DOGHOUSE REILLY

in

Sitting

Ducks

Other *Doghouse Reilly* books
by *Robin Kingsland*
in Red Fox

Donkeys Don't Just Die

Reilly's Rules

DOGHOUSE REILLY

in

Sitting Ducks

ROBIN KINGSLAND

RED FOX

A Red Fox Book

Published by Random House Children's Books
20 Vauxhall Bridge Road, London SW1V 2SA

A division of Random House UK Ltd
London Melbourne Sydney Auckland
Johannesburg and agencies throughout the world

Copyright © Robin Kingsland 1996

1 3 5 7 9 10 8 6 4 2

First published simultaneously in hardback and paperback by
The Bodley Head Children's Books and Red Fox 1996

This book is sold subject to the condition that it shall not, by way of
trade or otherwise, be lent, resold, hired out, or otherwise circulated
without the publisher's prior consent in any form of binding or cover
other than that in which it is published and without a similar condition
including this condition being imposed on the subsequent purchaser.

The right of Robin Kingsland to be identified as the author of this work
has been asserted by him in accordance with the Copyright, Designs
and Patents Act, 1988.

Set in Optima

Printed and bound in Great Britain by
Cox & Wyman Ltd, Reading, Berkshire

Papers used by Random House UK Ltd are natural, recyclable
products made from wood grown in sustainable forests. The
manufacturing processes conform to the environmental regulations of
the country of origin.

RANDOM HOUSE UK Limited Reg. No. 954009

ISBN 0 09 943351 6

20083986
MORAY COUNCIL
LIBRARIES &
INFORMATION SERVICES
JJC

Prologue

Years ago, the
story says, a train was
loaded with a cargo of
precious jewels. It was
loaded at night, in secret,
and it set off to a secret
destination. But somehow, word of the
treasure train reached the ruthless Toad in
the Hole gang, and they decided to help
themselves to its booty. So it happened that,
somewhere in the dark, the treasure train
vanished . . . into thin air.

No one knows how the gang managed to
steal a whole train, but they did, and spirited
it away to a secret hiding place. A map was made
of the hiding place, so that they could return
later and divide up the loot.

They never made it.

The police found the getaway truck, smashed to matchwood. The Toad in the Hole gang lay scattered like broken toys. Curiously enough, though, there was no sign of a map anywhere . . .

Chapter ①

And dey never found no treasure neither - no sir!

I first heard the story of Toad's Treasure from Mr Gippetto, who lives above me, soon after I moved into this neighbourhood. It was an old story then, and like most of these local stories, I assumed it was 100 per cent boloney . . .

Until a few weeks ago that is, when Milton J. Duckweed III arrived in my life . . .

I hadn't had a case in weeks and I was in a mean mood. I had spent the entire morning looking for the three Gruff brothers.

Fascinating.

They were in dispute with some guy about the right of way over a bridge and I wanted to offer my services. Anyway, by the time I got there, they had found their own solution to the problem. I was back to square one, which in my case is a little place the size of a shoebox, over by the railway.

I arrived at the shoebox, tired, grouchy and unemployed, to find some little squirt playing with my typewriter. He was small and fat, with two big

flat feet, and he wore a ridiculous sailor suit. As he heard me come in, he swung around. The typewriter crashed and fell onto the telephone. Then they both fell on my foot. Several pieces broke off — off the typewriter I mean, not my foot. There was an awkward silence.

'Can I do something for you, kid?' I said finally. 'Or did you just come in to break my equipment?'

The kid gave me a grin that was bigger than he was and said, 'Are you Mr Reilly? Mr Doghouse Reilly? Mr Reilly the detective?'

'That's my name, kid,' I said, 'don't wear it out.'

9

'Wow! I never met a real detective before. It's going to be swell staying with you.'

'Look, kid, I've had a heavy day so—' I stopped in mid-sentence and looked at him hard. 'Did you say "Staying with you"?' He nodded. Suddenly I felt as if I was in the wrong shoebox. 'Let's go back to the beginning,' I said.

Junior had evidently remembered something. Taking off his hat, he pulled a little wad of folded paper out of it. 'I have a note,' he said, holding it out to me. I took the note and read it.

Dear Mr Reilly,
This is to introduce Milton J. Duckweed III
His uncle, Drake Duckweed, is here on
business, and wants someone to
take care of Milton. Your
name was mentioned and I
said you'd be delighted.
Thank you, Reilly—it's only
for a few days,
H. T Dumpty.

I read the note twice — I didn't believe it the first time. H.T. Dumpty was asking me to baby-sit this . . . this . . . sawn-off sailor! Of course I couldn't really refuse. I owed Dumpty several favours, and this was obviously his way of evening up the score. But that didn't mean I had to be happy about it!

'OK, kid,' I said. 'Here are the ground rules: Don't touch anything, don't say anything and don't get under my feet. That way we will get along just fine.'

'Oh!' You could practically hear the kid's face hit the floor. 'I thought I could help you with your work.'

'I don't need any help,' I told him. I didn't mention that I didn't have any work, either. 'Look, kid,' I said. 'Why don't you go play outside?'

'Uncle Drake said I wasn't to go out on my own.'

Uncle Drake again!

'OK, OK,' I sighed. 'We'll *both* go for a walk.'

A walk would calm me down. Besides, there was someone I wanted to speak to — my old friend H.T. Dumpty.

Chapter 2

We walked to Dumpty's Club — the Wendy House. It wasn't far away, but it took forever to get there! Every few steps the kid would disappear round a corner, or into some building, and I'd have to go along and drag him out. As if that wasn't enough, we'd pass some bad-tempered local dinosaur, and Milton would practically yell, 'Look, Mr Reilly, a suspicious criminal type!'

We were lucky to reach the Wendy House without getting the stuffing knocked out of us.

I I.T. Dumpty was sitting at his usual table with Charley Taiwan, his bodyguard, and Miss Teers, the star singer at the club.

'Hi, Mr Dumpty!' Milton yelled. Everybody turned to look. I wanted the floor to open up and

swallow me. This kid was doing nothing for my
tough-guy image. Dumpty
and Co. could hardly
hide their giggles as I
came up to the table.

'Well, hello there Mr
Reilly!' the fat man
chuckled. 'I see you've
met Milton.' I grunted and
gave him my best I'll-get-
you-for-this look.

'Milton, what a fine name!' sang Miss Teers.
'Pleased to meet you, Milton.'

'How do you do, Miss Teers,' Milton simpered,
whisking his hat off. 'Gee, you're pretty.' I saw
Miss Teers' big blue eyes filling up.

14

That doll could sing like an angel . . .

. . . but she could also cry like Niagara Falls.

'Listen, Dumpty,' I said when the waterworks had stopped, 'just how long do I have to drag this kid around with me? He's a menace!'

'I like him!' Charley Taiwan smiled.

'Then you look after him!' I snapped.

'Come now, Reilly,' Dumpty said innocently. What's the problem?'

'I'll tell you what the problem is! So far he's broken my telephone, my typewriter, and my foot . . . and I've only known him for ten minutes! Truly Dumpty, I could kill him. And as for his uncle, if I ever get my hands on him I'll—'

'You'll what, Reilly?' said a voice behind me.

'I don't think you two have met,' said H.T. Dumpty. There was no question that *this* was Milton's uncle. Same shape, same profile, same feet – just bigger.

'Am I to understand that you don't like my nephew, Reilly?' Drake asked. You could have sliced bread with the edge in his voice. A little soft soap was called for.

'Me?' I cried. 'Not like Milton? Nonsense, we get on like a house on fire!'

Charley Taiwan looked puzzled. 'But Mr Reilly you just said—'

'Charley,' I said quickly, 'this is a private conversation. Shouldn't you be somewhere else, polishing your knuckles or something?' Charley fell silent. I turned back to Drake. 'Listen, Mr Duckweed. I'm not saying that Milton is a bad kid, but he is a kid, and I'm a busy detective.'

'Oh? I heard you hadn't had a case in weeks.' I shot a look at Dumpty. What a tattletale!

'I'm expecting a call at any moment,' I said.

'So you don't want to look after Milton any more?'

'No.'

'Are you sure? I could pay you, you know.' He mentioned an amount. My jaw dropped open like a trap door. It was a big amount. 'But, of course, if you're busy . . .'

'Well, when I say busy . . .'

'You're expecting a call!'

'I'll take the phone off the hook,' I said and gave him my sunniest smile.

'Then it's a deal, Mr Reilly,' said Drake Duckweed. 'Until further notice your only task is to look after young Milton. Now, my business is urgent, so I'll say goodbye.' And before I knew it, he was waddling out of the door.

'Just who does he think he is?' I growled.

'He thinks he's the head of the Duckweed Corporation,' Dumpty said. 'And he's right!'

'The Duckweed Corporation?'

'I'm surprised you haven't heard of it, Reilly. It's a

real rags-to-riches story. You see, years ago, Drake was a humble company secretary when he suddenly lost his job. Thrown on the scrap heap without a penny. But Drake Duckweed was a determined character. Within a year he had built a massive fortune, and the Duckweed Corporation was born!'

'And little Milton is his nephew?' I said.

'Well, not exactly,' Dumpty replied. 'Milton's father, Mallard Duckweed, was a distant relative of Drake's. When Milton was born, Drake said that if anything happened to Mallard, he would look after the kid. Then a couple of months ago, Mallard was involved in a freak accident with an elephant.' Dumpty's voice dropped to a whisper. 'Between you  and me, I don't think Drake is wild about having Milton around but, until they can find another living relative, Milton is his responsibility!'

'Except of course when he's MY responsibility!' I muttered.

'Oh cheer up, Reilly!' Dumpty exclaimed. 'Milton may be lively, but he's harmless. This will be the easiest money you'll ever earn. Why, if I were you . . .'

His attention was distracted by a tremendous crash in one corner of the Wendy House. A table had been overturned and customers stood dripping, complaining loudly as Miss Teers tried to calm them down, clean up and cry all at the same time. And there, in the middle of it all, was the cause of the disaster — Milton!

'Harmless, huh?' I said.

Dumpty cracked. 'Take that juvenile delinquent and get out of here!' he yelled.

'Hey, wait a minute!'

'You're responsible for him, Reilly! Get him out! Now!'

I grabbed Milton. 'Come with me,' I barked, 'before I bust your beak!'

BWAAH - WAAH!

There, there Miss Teers.

I had lost my patience and I decided to keep walking until I found it again. I could hear the kid flapping along behind me, trying to keep up. 'I'm really sorry,' he gabbled. 'But those people looked like suspicious criminal types.'

'Ha!' I said and kept going.

'I was only trying to help you, Mr Reilly.' His voice cracked and I heard a little sob.

I stopped and took a deep breath. 'I told you, kid. I don't need any help! Now try and stay out of trouble, and stay close, 'cos this is a rough neighbourhood!'

I turned.

Milton had gone. I couldn't believe this kid! 'Milton?' I called out. 'Hey, Duckweed?! Where are you?'

'I'm here, Mr Reilly!' He was standing stock still a little way behind me and his head was cocked away to one side.

'Milton!' I snapped, striding back to grab him. 'What are you doing?'

'I hear voices, Mr Reilly.'

I was just telling him that hearing voices is a sign of madness when I stopped. I was hearing voices too! There were two of them. One was low and growly. The other sounded tinny and rasping.

Instinct made me listen to their conversation. Apparently, Growler had paid a house call on Tinny, and now Tinny was accusing Growler of having stolen something while he was there.

'I know you took it!' Tinny squawked. 'Now give it back!'

'It wasn't yours in the first place,' Growler replied. 'You're winding me up, Nardo. Now hand it over!'

'Why don't you come and get it?'

That was when the fighting started. I turned to Milton. 'Stay here and don't move,' I barked, and ran around the corner.

Chapter 3

Tinny and Growler must have heard me coming, because by the time I got there, there was no sign of them.

It was dark in that place. Dark and eerily quiet after the noise of the shouting and scuffling. I peered into the gloom. I was tense, alert, ready for anything. Anything except the tug on my coat tail.

'Sorry, Mr Reilly. Did I scare you?'

'Of course you . . . er. . . didn't! Hey! What are

you doing here anyway? I thought I told you to stay put!' Milton looked up at me with those big eyes, but I wasn't about to give in. 'Look, kid,' I said firmly. 'Whoever it was, they're not here now. So let's go.'

'Mr Reilly.' Milton's voice was a whisper. He was looking past me, to a dark shadow beside a digger. I looked.

Someone was there, crouched in the pool of darkness.

'We can seeee you!' I sang. 'Come out, come out, whoever you are!'

A piece of the dark detatched itself and stepped sullenly forward.

'Don't tell me,' I said, 'you were just checking the oil, right?'

'It's none of your business what I was doing,' the stranger said. I could tell by the voice that this was the growler. Now, what was it the tinny-voiced one had called him. Oh yeah, that was it . . .

'You must be Nardo!' I said. He ignored me and felt in his pockets. Whatever was or wasn't in them must have upset him, because he snarled and began pacing around looking at the floor.

'Have you lost something, sir?' Milton asked.

'Be quiet, kid,' Nardo said.

'Hey!' I said. 'Don't talk to him like that, he's with me.'

'Thank you, Mr Reilly,' Milton beamed.

'Be quiet, kid,' I said.

Nardo looked up sharply. 'You're Reilly?' he snapped. 'Reilly the detective?'

I nodded.

'If you describe this whatever-it-is you're looking for,' I suggested helpfully, 'maybe we could help you look for it?' The look he gave me said a lot of things, but 'Thank you, that would be lovely' was not one of them.

'It doesn't matter,' he said at last. 'It's not important.'

'You could have fooled me,' I said.

'Maybe that's not hard to do,' he growled. And he turned and sloped off into the darkness.

'Aren't you going to go after him, Mr Reilly?' Milton gasped.

'No!' I said. 'I'm going home. It's late!'

'He was awfully rude to you.'

'Unfortunately, Milton, being awfully rude is not a crime. Now come on.'

'But, Mr Reilly,' Milton began, 'I'm sure he's a criminal type.'

I grabbed him and started to walk.

When we got back, I made up a little bed in a corner of the shoebox. 'OK, Milton,' I said. 'Hit the sack. You should have been asleep hours ago.'

'Oh, it's been such an exciting day, Mr Reilly,' he sighed, climbing under the sheet. 'I don't think I'll ever be able to sleep again!'

'Try. OK, kid. Just try.'

There was no reply. 'Are you listening, Milton?' I said . . .

But Milton J. Duckweed III wasn't listening. He was already far, far away and, if I knew anything about it, dreaming of 'criminal types'.

I got as comfortable as I could and pulled my hat low. 'Goodnight, kid,' I murmured, and shut my tired eyes.

Chapter 4

I spent the next morning fixing the typewriter.
Then I got Milton organised and we hopped into
my car and went to find my old friend Officer
McWheely.

'Well if it isn't the babysitter,'
McWheely chuckled when
we arrived.

'Very funny!' I said. 'Listen McWheely, did you
ever hear of a character named Nardo?'
The old cop scratched his head. 'Nardo. . .

Nardo . . . Sure, I remember now. He's a crook alright. Mainly small-time — you know, burglary, petty theft, that sort of thing. Why do you ask?'

I told him about our meeting the previous evening.

'Yep! That sounds like Nardo,' McWheely nodded. 'Maybe I should pay him a little call. You know, welcome him back to the neighbourhood! Why don't you follow me in the car!'

Ray Nardo lived in a shabby little box in a shabby little corner at the edge of the neighbourhood. The walls shook when McWheely knocked, but there was no answer.

'Nardo!' the big cop yelled. 'It's the police! Come on out!'

'I'll be right there, officer, sir,' a frail voice called.   McWheely and I waited . . .

    . . . and waited. . .

        . . . and waited.

'Come on, Nardo!' McWheely bellowed impatiently.

'Coming, officer!' the frail voice said.

I hardly recognised the figure that finally came hobbling out of the box. About all you could see were two ears and a snout. Everything else was bandaged.

'I'm sorry to have kept you waiting,' Nardo purred. His voice was as sweet as apple sauce. 'As you can see, I'm not too nimble at the moment. I had a little mishap a few days ago. Now, what seems to be the problem, officer?'

'A few days ago?' McWheely looked at me hard.

'You've been like this a few days?'

'Certainly.'

'Mr Reilly here says you were in a fight last night.'

'He must be mistaken. I haven't been out for days.' With his good arm he indicated his sling and splints. 'Walking is still quite painful.'

'You're lying!' I cried. 'You were fit as a fox last night and you had a major row with someone about stolen property. I heard you!'

Nardo ignored me and turned to McWheely. 'Can your . . . witness name this other person? Can he describe him? Can he describe the stolen property that we were supposed to be fighting over?'

McWheely glared at me as I was forced to shake my head to every question.

'Then if you've no further questions, officer, I need to rest this leg.' Nardo threw in a wince for good measure.

Moving away a little, McWheely motioned me to join him. He was not happy.

'You surely don't believe all this baloney?' I gasped.

'It doesn't matter if I believe him or not! You've got no evidence. You're just letting him make us both look stupid! Now why don't you—'

The noise pulled us both round. Milton had leapt forward, snarling. He was practically standing on

Nardo's chest.
  'You're hiding

something,
Nardo!' he yelled.
'And we're going to
find out what. You may say
you weren't there last night, but
me and my partner know better!
We don't know what your little caper is
yet, but I tell you this. We . . .'
He didn't say any more.
Oh, he wanted to, but
somehow. . . the
words wouldn't
come.

MMMLLFF!!!

'OK, Nardo,' McWheely said. 'We'll leave it at that for now, but I'll be watching you.' 'And so will I,' I added. Nardo turned his narrow eyes on me. 'Gee,' he sneered, 'I'm sooo scared!'

'You shouldn't have stopped me, Mr Reilly!' Milton wailed, when I finally got him back to the shoebox. 'A little more pressure and he would have sung like a canary.'

'Kid,' I growled, 'I could cheerfully wring your neck! When are you going to learn to stay out of trouble, huh? When?'

'I was only trying to help, Mr Reilly. I thought together we could get the truth out of him. I think we make a great team.'

'Listen, Milt,' I said, as gently as I could, 'you're a nice kid, and I know you mean well, and I don't want to hurt your feelings but,

That did it. He looked up at me and two big, fat tears rolled slowly down his face.

And that was the scene that greeted Drake Duckweed as he arrived.

Chapter 5

'I'm disappointed in you, Reilly,' Drake said. 'Dumpty assured me that you would treat my nephew well.'

'Hey!' I said. 'We're getting along just dandy! Isn't that right, Milton?' I gave the kid a friendly hug. Instantly the tears stopped and Milton looked up at me. There was no mistaking that look. I was his hero. I felt so guilty, I wanted the floor to open up and swallow me. Drake wasn't satisfied, though.

'I've been hearing things, Reilly. Things that I don't like. I hear you've been taking Milton with you on your detective work.'

'Well I . . .' How had he found out so soon, I wondered? That blabbermouth McWheely, presumably.

'I have paid you handsomely to look after my nephew,' Drake snapped. 'Not to drag him around on your unsavoury cases.' I tried to protest, but he stopped me. 'Our agreement was quite clear, Mr Reilly. Stay away from detective work until my business is finished and Milton returns to my care. Is that understood?'

He didn't wait to find out if it was understood or not. He just turned and flapped out.

'You mustn't let Uncle upset you, Mr Reilly,' Milton said. 'He can be a little bossy at times.'

'Sure,' I muttered, 'and the Sahara Desert is a little dry.'

'Mr Reilly, I'm sorry I got you into trouble.' Milton hit me with the big eyes again.

'Forget it, Milton,' I sighed. 'Trouble is my middle name.'

'Really?! That's unusual. My middle name is—'

I leaned out to see
McWheely down below.
'McWheely!' I cried.
'How've you been? I
haven't seen you for, oooh,
at least an hour!'
'Cut the wisecracks,
Reilly,' the cop said. 'I've
just had a call from Roli.
Someone tried to kill him!'
'NO! When?'
'About ten minutes ago.'
Roli Poli was an old
friend of mine. He used to
be a boxer but he was
retired now. He didn't
have an enemy in the
world, as far as I knew. So
who would try to kill him?
'I'll be right down,'
I yelled.

'But, Mr Reilly!' Milton cried. 'Uncle Drake
said—'

'I know what Uncle Drake said: He said I wasn't
to take you out on detective work. Well, a.) this
isn't detective work. I'm simply going to see an
old friend.'

'OK, Mr Reilly,' Milton grinned, 'I'll get my hat.'

'That's the b.) part,' I said. 'I'm not taking you with me.'

'But . . .'

'But nothing,' I said firmly. 'Stay here and don't touch anything

Especially the typewriter!

I hadn't seen Roli in quite a while. And life had obviously not been too lush lately.

He was living in the very worst part of the neighbourhood. Locals called it 'the darks'. Once you moved into this place, you did nothing but gather dust. It was sad to see a once-noble figure like Roli Poli here, and he looked in bad shape after his attack. He was standing up, but then, that's what had made him such a good boxer. No matter what you hit him with, he always stood up again.

'How's it going, Roli?' I said.

'Oh you know, Mr R., still duckin' and weavin'.'

'Yeah, well you didn't duck fast enough last night, Roli old pal,' McWheely said. 'That's a nasty crack on your noggin.'

'Dey hit me wid a big stick, I think, Mr McWheely,' the old bruiser said. 'Dey come up from behind me, udderwise I'd a had 'em!' He swung around to demonstrate. He was still pretty fast.

'Why would they want to hit you, Roli?' I asked.

'I don't know, Mr R.,' Roli said. He was puzzled. A lifetime of being knocked about had shaken a few parts loose in his head. 'I don't know, but I reckon it's on account of what I saw.'

'And what was that?'

'I saw them shaking my neighbour, Mr Reilly. They was being real rough. And den my neighbour he lay down like he was real tired or something.' McWheely and I looked at each other. We were both hearing the same warning bells. The big cop edged away to investigate. 'I shouted at them to stop. I said to leave my neighbour alone to sleep, and den one of the guys, he ran away. And when I chased him, the other one musta hit me from behind. That ain't fair, Mr Reilly — hitting a guy from behind.'

'Reilly?' McWheely called. 'Over here.'

I told Roli to stay put, and joined McWheely, already sure of what I'd find. Roli's neighbour was lying down all right. Trouble was, he was lying down in several places at once.

Whoever Roli had seen had done a real number on him, and what's more, they'd ransacked the little box he lived in.

'Whoever did this was looking for something,' I said.

'Yeah,' McWheely agreed. 'But what?'

'Who was this neighbour of yours, Roli?' I called out.

Roli said he didn't know. The guy had only moved in a couple of days ago. I started looking around for identification, while McWheely got on his radio to call for an ambulance. He looked again at the mess.

Er...
Better make
that a dumper
truck.

I had finally found some identification.

I asked McWheely if
the name meant anything
to him. He shook his head.

I took a last look at the remains of Tin Pot Ted.
Then I went back to ask Roli a few more
questions. I was in for a shock.

'Hi, Mr Reilly!'

'Milton! What the — what are you doing here?!'
Somehow he had got hold of a magnifying glass
and was scouring the scene of the crime.

'Go home!' I commanded.

'But I thought you might need help,' Milton said.

It was the last straw. I strode towards him.

'Don't send me away, Mr Reilly. I've already found some clues outside. Look.' He held up a sweet wrapper. I took it and shoved it in my pocket. 'And there's another thing . . .' he went on, but by this time I had him by the collar.

'Whatever it is you've found, I don't want to know. So just keep it under your hat and go home.'

You had to hand it to Milton, he didn't give up. In one swift waddle he ducked under my arm and got to Roli before I could grab him. 'Are you Mr Roli?' he asked. 'Is this Mr Roli, Mr Reilly?'

'Yes . . . No . . . Yes . . . Never mind. I told you to go!'

'I know but—'

'But nothing! Go back now!'

'I thought maybe if Mr Roli could describe what he saw I could do a picture. An artist's impression.'

I dragged Milton out of earshot. 'Listen,' I hissed, 'Roli is a nice guy, but a little underweight in the brain department. He can't remember his own name half the time, let alone—'

'Hey!' Roli suddenly lit up. 'That's a great idea, ain't it, Mr Reilly? I could tell the kid what the guy I chased looked like and he could draw it!'

I looked at Roli, dumbfounded. Then I looked at Milton's big eyes beaming up at me.

'Er . . . just what I was about to suggest, Roli,' I called. 'Let's get back to McWheely's and get some paper!'

Milton's style was a little rough around the edges, but the picture he drew from Roli's description was enough for me. I showed it to McWheely.

'Add a couple of bandages and a sling and what have you got?' I said.

McWheely nodded slowly. 'I think tomorrow we pay another visit to Mr Ray Nardo,' he said.

All that drawing had tired Milton out. I had to practically carry him to the car. Then I had to heave him up to the shoebox. By the time that was done I was feeling dead-beat too. But there was no rest for Reilly. Just as I started to nod off, Milt started jabbering.

Mmmble.... mmble... Look what I found... Everybody wants... what should I... what if.... w... mmmmm...

Gradually, the muttering subsided . . . only to start up again a couple of minutes later. I settled down again. A couple of minutes later:

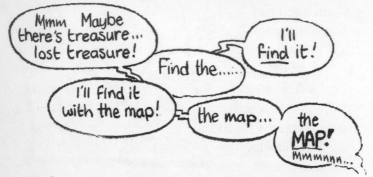

And so it went on, every two or three minutes. After an hour, I couldn't stand it any more. I went to find somewhere else to sleep.

You know when a postman tries to push a big parcel through a small letter box? Well, when I woke up next morning, I knew exactly how those parcels feel. I was crumpled, rumpled and mean.

'Good morning, Mr Reilly,' Milton said, as I crawled back into the shoebox. He might as well have lit the blue touch paper. I went off like a Roman candle.

'It is not a good morning, kid! I have just spent the night folded up like a Sunday paper! I have aches where I didn't even know I had places. And it's your fault. Stay away from me, don't talk to me, and most of all, do not say dumb things to me like "Good morning".'

'Good morning,' Milton said.

'I'm warning you, kid!'

'Oh, I wasn't speaking to you, Mr Reilly. I was speaking to Uncle Drake.'

I turned around slowly. There was Uncle Drake, as large as life. This was turning into such a bad day, and it had hardly even begun.

As usual, Drake didn't beat around the bush. 'I've been hearing things, Mr Reilly. Things that concern me very much. You took Milton into the most unsavoury neighbourhood—'

'I didn't take him. He—'

'Don't interrupt, Mr Reilly. You took Milton on a case when I paid you not to. You exposed my nephew to grave dangers. I begin to wonder whether my trust in you was justified.'

That was too much. The old blue touch paper started fizzing again. 'If that's how you feel,

Duckweed, find yourself another nursemaid. Milton's a nice, good, friendly kid, but I never asked for him — you forced him onto me. If you want to take him back now, that's just fine!' I rummaged around and found the wad of notes he had given me. 'Here's your money. Count it if you like.'

We stood there for a few moments. I could sense Milton watching us and I knew without looking that those big tears would be getting ready to roll.

Abruptly, Drake Duckweed's manner changed. He relaxed and came as close to smiling as I'd ever seen. 'Now, Mr Reilly,' he said soothingly. 'I'm sorry if I offended you. Believe me, my only concern is Milton's wellbeing.'

'Yeah. Well I'm sorry too,' I said. 'I shouldn't have lost my temper. I didn't get much sleep last night. Junior here was talking in his sleep. Yakking about maps, or hidden treasure or something,' I laughed.

'The kid's obviously been reading too many comic books.'

'Indeed,' Drake said vaguely. He was looking past me at Milton. He started to say something, then looked at me and changed his mind. Instead he said, 'Mr Reilly, I suspect I may wrap things up here sooner than I thought. Keep this money and I will see that Milton is off your hands soon. Very soon. Agreed?'

I nodded and Drake left without another word. I watched him go, then turned to find Milton right behind me, with a face longer than a freight train.

'Mr Reilly,' he said quietly, 'I got you into terrible trouble. Maybe . . .' he sniffed and wiped his eyes. 'Maybe I should have gone with Uncle Drake.'

'Ah listen, kid,' I said, putting my arm around him. 'Those things I said, they were just talk. I know you don't mean any harm. Why, when I was your age, I was exactly the same.'

'You were?' Suddenly he brightened up

'Sure I was!'

'Oh, Mr Reilly. I promise I'll be good from now on. I'll even stay here this morning when you go out.'

'When I go out? I'm not going anywhere.'

'Weren't you and Officer McWheely going to see Mr Nardo today?'

NARDO!!? I'd forgotten all about him! 'I've got to run!' I yelled. 'Listen, kid, if you get bored, Mr Gippetto lives right above me. Get him to tell you some of his stories.'

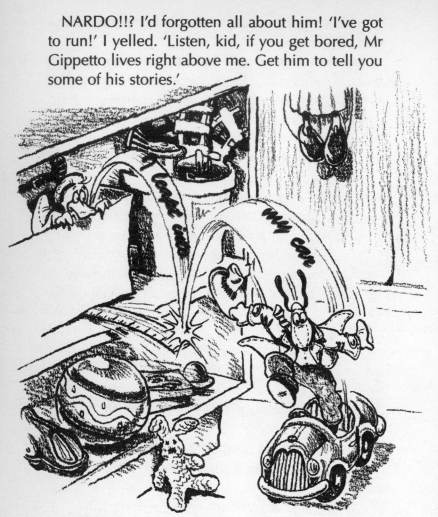

I leapt into my car, drove like a demon and managed to catch up with McWheely just as he arrived at Nardo's place. We found Nardo sitting outside.

'Where were you last night, Nardo?' McWheely asked, taking out Milton's picture.

'Right here,' Nardo said. He tapped the splints on his leg. 'Where else am I going to go like this?'

'So you didn't take a little stroll to Tin Pot Ted's place?'

'I've never even heard of him.'

McWheely unrolled the picture with a flourish.

'This is an artist's impression of someone seen running from the scene. It looks like you.'

'Could be anybody,' Nardo sneered. 'It ain't exactly Michelangelo! Besides,' he smiled, 'look at this leg. Whoever was running last night, it wasn't me!'

Something had been bothering me. Suddenly I

knew what it was. 'You know, it's a funny thing,' I said casually. 'I could have sworn you had that sling on the other arm yesterday!'

'Hey!' McWheely said slowly. 'You're right, Reilly. It *was* on the other arm!'

Ray Nardo's free hand reached into his arm sling. A moment later it reappeared together with a pretty ugly addition.

'OK. Get those hands up,' Nardo commanded.

'Let me guess, Ray,' I said, as Nardo shrugged off his fake bandages. 'Tin Pot Ted was the guy you fought with the other night, right? He managed to get back whatever it was you'd stolen, so you set up the "injury" scam to give you an alibi in advance. But Ted was too smart for you, wasn't he? He'd hidden the whatever-it-was. So you decided to bump him off!'

'Hey! Wait!' All of a sudden, Nardo wasn't so confident. 'I . . . I never killed nobody.'

'Then who did, Nardo? Who killed Tin Pot Ted?'

'You think I'd tell you? And then what? I'm the next one dead, that's what.' Ray came slowly towards us. 'You poor dummies,' he said. 'You think you're so smart, but you don't even know what you're dealing with here. Take my advice, both of you. Forget last night, forget you ever saw me and forget you ever heard of Toad's Treasure. That way you might just stay healthy.'

'Toad's Treasure?' McWheely gasped. 'What's Toad's Treasure got to do with this?'

Nardo realised he'd said too much. Now he looked really scared. 'Turn around,' he barked, 'and start counting. If you move before you reach one hundred, you'll regret it as long as you live — which won't be very long!'

I started counting, nice and slow. I heard the hoppity hoppity noise of Ray limping away. 'Eight, nine, ten . . .'

'Let's go after him,' McWheely whispered. 'He can't get far with those splints on his leg.' At that moment, my car clattered past, with Ray Nardo at the wheel. He hurtled

EEEEEEEEEEEEEEE

EEEEEEK!

around the corner and disappeared.

'You were saying,' I sighed.

We counted up to thirty, then McWheely started getting stuck so we gave up. 'I'd better get back to headquarters,' the big cop said, 'and put out a description of that creep.' Revving his bike up, he swung round and rode quickly away. I heard his siren fade into the distance.

I sat down and tried to think. I knew now that Ray Nardo had a boss somewhere. A boss he was scared of. And whatever it was that Ray's boss had been after, he had been prepared to take Tin Pot Ted apart to get it. But what was it? And what did it have to do with that old fairy story of Toad's Treasure? I didn't know, but I was sure going to try to find out! I just had to hope that Milton's Uncle Drake didn't get to hear about it!

Talking of Milton, it was time I got back. I stood up, brushed myself down, and turned for home.

That was when I saw him. There was no mistaking the tubby little figure in the sailor suit: Milton J. Duckweed III. He was still some distance away, when he spotted me. 'Mr Reilly!' he called out. 'I came as soon as I got your message.'

'Message?' I said. 'I didn't leave any . . .' I felt a cold shiver and all the hairs on the back of my neck rose. I started to run towards the kid. 'Milton!' I yelled. 'Go back! Get down! Get out of the way.'

A big dark car came screaming out of nowhere. If I hadn't dived out of the way, it would have mown me down.

'RUN KID!' I shouted. But it was too late. Milton stood, dumbly bewildered, as the car squealed to a halt beside him.

I saw him grabbed and pulled in. There was a high-pitched whine from the engine before the car finally screeched away again.

Then there was nothing to hear but silence and nothing to see but Milton's sailor hat, lying where it had fallen. I picked it up and put it in my pocket and wondered how much worse this day could get.

Much, much worse was the answer.

Chapter 6

The Crooked Man
is going straight!

This is ridiculous!' I yelled. 'You can't arrest me!
Why I was almost killed myself!'

Mona Lisa was framed. Leo.

I was in the slammer. How did I get in there?
Simple. Drake Duckweed had had me arrested on
possible charge of murder. And who, you might ask,
was the suspected victim? You guessed it, Milton J.
Duckweed III. As he was now missing
his uncle had kindly suggested that I,
who had cared for Milton for so
long, had now done him in and
conveniently disposed of the body!
'McWheely,' I pleaded. 'You don't
really believe I'd harm the kid.'
'I don't know, Reilly,' McWheely
sighed. He held up a sheaf of
statements.

'There's a lot of people here who heard you threaten him. Listen, some Russian Doll claims you told her you could "cheerfully strangle the little geek!"; several witnesses at the Wendy House heard you threaten to "Bust his Beak"; and Mr Gippetto says he overheard you say to Milton "I'll wring your neck!". It looks bad, Reilly!'

'A lot of people say "I'll wring your neck!" McWheely. If you're going to arrest them all, it's going to get pretty crowded in here. It's just something you say when you're mad.'

'I'm sorry, Reilly.' McWheely shook his head. 'If someone else could back up your kidnapping story . . .'

The Knave of Hearts is Innocent

He had a point. There were no other witnesses to back me up.

'Listen, McWheely. Do you trust me?'

'Sure I do, Reilly, but . . .'

'Then do me a favour. This kidnapping has got to be tied up with the Ray Nardo thing. I don't know what the connection is, but if you could let me out for a couple of hours . . .'

'I can't do that, Reilly.'

'Two hours, McWheely! If I can't clear my name by then I promise I'll come back.'

'But Mr Duckweed would have me suspended.'

'So don't tell him. Come on, McWheely. You know I'm as good as my word. Two hours from now I'll be back here.'

McWheely squirmed. I knew I was putting him in a tough position, but I was in an even tougher one. 'Two hours? You promise?'

'Scout's honour.'

After a long, long pause, McWheely finally nodded. I fell out of the slammer and pumped his hand. 'Two hours isn't long, Reilly,' the big cop

said. 'Good luck . . . you'll
need it.'

'Thanks, McWheely,' I
called over my shoulder.
'You won't regret this.'

'I already do,' I heard
him say.

I was looking for a needle in a haystack and I didn't
even know where the haystack was. I headed back
to the shoebox, keeping close against walls,
walking in the shadows in case the police saw me.
They were crawling all over, looking for Ray Nardo,
I hoped. One time I nearly got spotted, coming
around the corner as a patrol car was coming the
other way, but I managed
to hide myself.

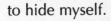

WEE OOooo
WEE OOooo
WEE OOooo

When I got to the shoebox, I found the police had been there already. They'd taken everything. I sat in the empty box and plunged my paws into my pockets and felt one of them close on Milton's little sailor hat. I took it out and straightened it. Strange, all the time he'd been there I'd wanted to get rid of him. Now I wanted more than anything to find him again.

I flung the hat into a corner and cursed myself. It was my fault he'd been kidnapped. Now he was missing, perhaps even — no! I wouldn't let myself think like that. I was going to find Milton J. Duckweed III, if it was the last thing I did.

My thoughts were interrupted by the sound of Mr Gippetto calling my name softly. He must have seen me sneak in. Obviously my sneaking abilities were a litte rusty. 'Hi, Mr Gippetto.'

'Mr Reilly, the police said you vos — how do you say it — in de slammer.'

'I still am, at least I'm supposed to be. So do me a favour, Mr G., and pretend you never saw me.'

'Me?' he said in mock surprise. 'I never saw nobody. My eyes, they ain't so good!'

'You're a pal, Mr Gippetto.'

'Ach! Mr Reilly.' Mr Gippetto let out a long sigh. 'I hear about dat poor little kid, dat Milton. I can't beliff he's gone. I vos only talking to him today, telling him a few stories. It vos just before he went to see Admiral Cyclops.'

'Wait a minute!' I cried, instantly snapping out of my misery. 'Milton went to see The Admiral?? When? Why?'

Admiral Cyclops was a one-eyed old sea-dog about a million years old. He had a place high up overlooking the neighbourhood.

No one visited him and as far as anyone knew, he never moved. He just sat up there looking down on all of us with his one, glassy eye. Of all people, why had Milton gone to see him?

The answer, apparently, was Mr Gippetto. He'd told Milton stories all right. Funny ones, sad ones and then, of course, he'd got on to the story of Toad's Treasure. 'Suddenly, the kid's eyes light up like he's baddery operated or somesing and ven I finish, he asks me is de story true.'

'What did you tell him, Mr G?'

'I told him I don't know. I told him you have to ask somevun who lived here a long time — somevun like the Admiral! Then he vent away and ven he come back, there vos your message.' When I told him that I hadn't sent the message, Mr Gippetto's hands flew to his face. 'Mama mia,' he said softly.

'Mr Gippetto,' I asked. 'Did you see anyone come here after Milton left?'

'I'm sorry, Mr Reilly, I vos tired after all those stories. I fell asleep. I only voke when the kid came back. By then, the note, it vos there.'

I thanked him and left. Plunging into the shadows again, I made my way towards the Admiral's place. My mind was in turmoil. Somehow everything was starting to connect, but not in any way that made sense. A police car wailed past. I pushed myself into a corner till it had gone.

NEE
NAW
NEE
NAW
NEE
NAW
NEE
NAW
NEE
NAW

Connections. Connections. Toad's Treasure. Ray Nardo had warned us to forget it, before we'd even mentioned it. Milton had suddenly become interested when Mr Gippetto had mentioned it. Two separate people showing a sudden interest in an old bedtime story was more than coincidence. So, what if the story had some truth to it, I thought? What if Toad's Treasure really exists? That would explain Nardo's angle. But Milton was new to the neighbourhood. He'd never heard of Toad's Treasure until today. So why was he interested? And then there was the biggest puzzle of all — what could anybody gain by snatching the kid?

Ah...
This must be it.

After a long climb, I reached Admiral Cyclops'
place. I had heard a lot about this old guy, I had
even seen him from time to time, looking down
from up here. But this was the first time I'd met
him face to face. 'Admiral Cyclops, sir,' I began.
'My name is . . .'

'I know who you are, son,' the Admiral bragged.
'You're Reilly, the Detective!' Well, I thought, he
might be losing his hair, but his marbles are all in
place. 'This is quite an occasion, Reilly!'

'Sir?'

'I never normally get visitors way up here. Then
I get two in one day. I assume you've come about
young Duckweed.'

I nodded. 'Excuse me for asking, Admiral, but did Milton come asking you about the Toad's Treasure legend?'

'Yes he did. But it's no legend, Reilly. That train really existed. Really disappeared too. The darndest business. I told young Duckweed all I could remember, which is a lot, I can tell you.'

'I'm sure it is, sir. Er . . . Would you mind telling me too?'

The old Admiral told me everything. Most of it I'd heard before. But then something came up that was new. One of Toad's gang had survived, but before the police could catch him, he escaped to another area. 'Last I heard,' growled the Admiral, 'he'd been arrested for some other crime and sent to the local slammer.'

'Can you recall his name, sir?'

The Admiral scratched his grizzly head. 'Now, let me think. Fred . . . Jed . . . Ned . . . something like that.'

'Could it have been *Ted*, sir?' I asked. 'Tin Pot Ted?'

'That's the fella,' the Admiral cried. 'You know him?'

'No, but I can tell you one thing, he's not a survivor any more. He was killed the other night. Thanks, Admiral. You've been a great help.'

'Any time, Reilly.' I turned to go, but Admiral Cyclops wasn't finished with me yet. 'Want to know another curious thing, Reilly?' I turned back. 'There was a young fellow running the train-company office on the night of the robbery. Lost his job for losing the train. Want to know his name?' I nodded. 'Duckweed,' the Admiral said. 'Drake Duckweed. Small world isn't it?'

The Admiral was right. It was a small world. But it certainly wasn't a simple one. In fact it seemed to be getting more complicated by the minute. Was there anyone who wasn't connected with this case?

It was too risky to go back to the shoebox. I found a telephone and called McWheely. 'Reilly? What are you calling me for?' He sounded nervous.

'I need to talk, McWheely. Can you meet me somewhere?'

'Well . . . OK. But I'll be putting my neck on the line!'

'Mine's on the block already, McWheely.'

'OK. OK! The Wendy House. Five Minutes!'

I made my way to the Wendy House and let myself in the back way. The first person I saw was Charley Taiwan.

'Psst, Charley!' I whispered.

'Hey, Mr Reilly!' the big ape roared. 'It's good to see you.'

'Charley, please!' I begged. 'Could you lower your voice? Now, tell me, is Mr Dumpty in?' Charley's lips moved. 'What did you say, Charley?' I asked. The lips moved again. 'Huh? Can't you speak up?'

'But you told me—'

'Never mind what I told you Charley! Is Mr Dumpty in?'

Suddenly Dumpty was beside us. 'What's all the noise out here?' he snapped. Then he saw me. 'Why, Mr Reilly. We heard you were—'

'In the slammer? I was . . . I am . . . that is . . . It's a long story. Tell me, H.T.,' I asked, changing the subject, 'do you know anything about Toad's Treasure?'

'I know the old legend,' the fat man said.

'What if I told you it was no legend.'

H.T.'s eyes went saucer-sized as I told him about my meeting with the Admiral. I also told him what I'd found out about Drake Duckweed; how Duckweed had lost his job and his reputation after the robbery.

'He said he was in the neighbourhood on business,' I said finally. 'Do you know what kind of business?'

Dumpty shrugged.

'Shall I tell you what I think?' I declared. 'I think Drake Duckweed heard that Tin Pot Ted had got out of the slammer and that he was on his way back to try and find Toad's Treasure. Drake decided to track him down and find the treasure first, to clear his name after all these years. The trouble is, Ray Nardo and his boss beat him to it. Now Drake's going after them. You see? That's why Milton's been snatched. They're trying to get Drake off their backs by holding Milton hostage!'

Miss Teers and Charley had appeared. 'Oh that poor child!' Miss Teers wailed.

'Dumpty,' I said, 'do you know where I can find Drake Duckweed?'

Charley tapped me on the shoulder. 'Are you still on the run, Mr Reilly?'

'Yes, Charley. Why do you ask?'

''Cos a policeman just walked in.'

I jumped up so fast I lost my balance and crashed into the wall. I struggled to get up, but my feet seemed to have swapped places, or got tangled up somewhere. I heard a deep, growling chuckle. 'Is this what they mean by "lying low", Reilly?'

I clambered up and dusted myself down.

'McWheely,' I said. 'I'm glad you're here. We have to find Drake Duckweed.'

'Drake Duckweed!' The big cop looked surprised. 'He's the last person you want to see.'

'Seriously, McWheely. He's in danger.'

I told him my theory. McWheely frowned. 'I knew it was a mistake letting you out. Trouble comes to you like ants to a sandwich.' He sighed.

'OK,' he said. 'We'll go find him, but I do the talking. Understood?' I nodded and we left. It made a nice change to be going out the front way.

'I hope you know what you're doing,' McWheely muttered. 'Because I don't.'

I was about to answer him when we heard running footsteps. I ducked back into the shadows.

'Who is it?' I whispered.

'Son of a gun!' McWheely breathed. 'It's Ray Nardo! And he's heading this way.'

'Maybe he hasn't seen you,' I suggested. But Ray had seen the big cop. He ran straight up to him.

'Help me, McWheely!' he wheezed. 'You gotta help me. He's after me!'

I stepped out, forgetting the danger I was in. This was one scared individual, and I wanted to know what he was scared of.

'Who?' I demanded. 'Who's after you, Nardo? Your boss?' But Nardo was gabbling.

It was OK when we were just after Toad's Treasure, but then he bumped off Tin Pot Ted, and I started to get scared... ...and now, he's got the kid!

'Milton?' I said sharply.

Nardo nodded frantically. 'He says if the kid doesn't say where the map is he'll kill him. I may be a crook, Reilly, but I don't hold with killing. I said I'd had enough and now he's after me. You've got to help me. Protect me.'

'Who from?' I shook him. 'Who's your boss, Nardo?'

'You mean you don't know?' Nardo said. 'It's—'

I didn't even hear the gun. I just felt Nardo slump against me and fall to the ground. McWheely looked around, then revved up his bike and roared off in search of whoever had fired. In a few minutes he was back. 'Nardo?' he asked. 'Is he . . .' I nodded. 'Too bad. What was he saying about a map?'

It had been puzzling me, too. I thought about it. Three or four things suddenly started to make a weird kind of sense. I felt a tingle in the back of my neck. The tingle I always felt when I was close to solving a case. 'Didn't the old legend talk about a map to show where the train had been hidden?' McWheely nodded. 'And when we were talking to Roli Poli and Milton turned up, he said he'd found something.'

'Yeah, yeah,' the cop growled. 'I remember now.'

'I didn't take any notice at the time,' I said. 'I was too mad at him for turning up. But then that night, in his sleep, he talked about a map. I could kick myself! That's what Nardo and his boss have been after all along.'

'And now they've got Milton,' McWheely snarled.

'But not the map!' I said. A frown crossed McWheely's great forehead.

'So who does have the map?'

'Let me think,' I said. 'Just let me think.'

I tried to re-run everything that had happened in my head. Conversations tumbled through my mind. 'When Milton said he'd found something, I said . . . er . . . "throw it away". . . No! I said . . . "Put it away". . . No! I said . . . I said . . .' Suddenly I went cold. 'His hat!' I cried.

'His what?'

'That's why they haven't got the map. Because I told Milton to keep it *under his hat!!*'

McWheely was talking, but I wasn't listening. I started to run back to my place. It was still there, lying in a corner of the shoebox — Milton's little sailor hat. I felt inside it and my paw closed on a wad of folded paper. Trembling, I opened it up. There it was, old and yellowing; a map showing exactly where Toad's Treasure lay.

Only one thing still puzzled me. How did Nardo's boss know Milton had found this? Milton hadn't even told me, except when he talked in his sleep and I'd never mentioned that to anyone, except . . . For the second time I went cold all over. I *had* told someone about Milton talking in his sleep.

I had told Drake Duckweed.

So that was it! How could I have been so wrong? Drake wasn't in town to clear his name. He was here to get the treasure, the way he should have all those years ago, when, as a humble railway clerk, he had tipped off the Toad in the Hole gang about the jewel consignment. Drake had been behind the robbery all along. Drake was Nardo's big boss. Drake had killed Nardo and Tin Pot Ted! Drake had kidnapped little Milton! I had to get back to McWheely. I had to warn him.

I turned . . . and found myself staring down the barrel of a gun.

Going somewhere, Mr Reilly?

DART-O MATIC

'Well, Mr Reilly, we meet again.' Drake Duckweed was standing there, large as life. One hand held the gun; the other held Milton.

'Are you OK, Milton?' I asked. 'Has he hurt you?' Milton shook his head, but his eyes told their own story. Fear, surprise, confusion. It was hard to see which feeling was winning in there.

'You've been extremely troublesome to me, Reilly,' Drake said. 'Though I suppose I should thank you for finding the map! Dumpty is always telling me what a good detective you are. That's why I wanted you to look after Milton here. I thought it would keep you both out of my way. I was wrong.'

'You're making a big
mistake, Duckweed,' I
said, trying to stay cool.
'My neighbour is nosy.
He's probably called the
cops by now.'

Drake didn't flinch.
'You mean Mr Gippetto?'
he said. 'I think you'll
find he's a little tied up at
the moment.'

'You see I really do think of everything.'

'You always were ambitious, weren't you,
Drake,' I said. 'Even when you were a humble
company secretary. I can see how tempting it must
have been, when you were trusted with the secret
of the jewel cargo.

No one was in a better position to tell Toad's gang. You got greedy and did a deal, but it all went wrong, didn't it? The map went missing and your share of the loot with it. But you were prepared to wait.

Wait for Tin Pot Ted to come out of jail. You knew he had to have the map, because he was the only surviving member of Toad's gang. And so you waited all this time to hire Ray Nardo to steal it back.'

'Mr Reilly, I'm impressed. You're even smarter than I thought. Much too smart to live, unfortunately!'

'Just one question,' I said. 'You're obviously rich. The Duckweed Corporation has made you more money than you could ever spend. You took huge risks, killed two people and for what? To get treasure you don't even need. Why, Duckweed? Why did you do it?'

'Simple, Reilly,' Duckweed said. 'I don't like losing. And now, I must regretfully bring this interview to an end. I have a train to catch. Come with me, please, and don't try anything heroic.'

'Where are we going, Duckweed?'

'You'll see,' said Drake with a thin smile.

Chapter 8

I'd never even seen this place before. It was a water container of some kind, an enormous open tank, with a huge valve at one end. Drake held the gun on me while I tied Milton, then Drake tied my hands and feet. Just for good measure he tied weights to our legs. Then, with a shove,

he sent us slithering to the bottom

He ran to of one
of the great taps
and twisted it.
Cold water came
gushing down.
'Thank you for
all your help, Mr
Reilly!' Drake
yelled over the roar
of the water. 'I'm
sorry I can't stay for
the finale, but do
enjoy your dip.'
Then he was gone.

The moment Drake turned his back, I started struggling to free myself. At the same time I struggled to get upright. On a smooth, curved surface, tied up and weighted down, believe me it's not easy. Try it some time . . . On second thoughts, don't.

Not only was Drake Duckweed a crook and a killer and a wicked uncle, he also tied a pretty mean knot. The water was icy cold, and rising fast. It looked like curtains for Reilly. I glanced across to see how Milton was doing.

He was giving me that look again. That big-eyed, you're-my-hero look. It probably saved our lives. It kick started me. How could I let the kid down when he looked at me that way? I threw myself into the struggle once more, and . . .

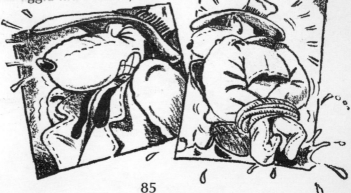

I got my feet free and waded over to Milton. I reached him just as his head was going under and freed him.

'Now, kid, you swim across to—'

'I can't swim, Mr Reilly.'

'Don't interrupt, Milton, we don't have—'

'I can't swim. I'm the only one in our family

who can't. I guess I'm just not made of the right stuff. I'm sorry.'

'That's great. Just GREAT.'

'Can't *you* swim, Mr Reilly.'

'Er – no.'

'Well, it's been nice knowing you, Mr Reilly.'

That was when I spotted the chain. It ran down into the water to a bung of some sort. It was big, but with the two of us pulling . . . I was just keeping my nose above water now. There wasn't much time. Milton clambered onto my shoulders and I started to wade. My legs seemed to weigh a ton.

The chain hung directly under the gushing water. 'OK, Milton!' I yelled, as the water thundered down. 'On the count of three, pull! One . . . two

. . . THREE!'
We pulled. Nothing happened.

'Again! One . . . two . . . THREE!'
We pulled. Nothing happened.

'Again! One . . . two . . . THREE!'

We pulled. The bung stayed put, but the water rose further.

'Again!' We pulled. The plug stayed in . . . but had I felt it shift? The water was up to my ears now.

'Pul-bblebrrbble!!' I managed to yell as my mouth went under.

We both fell back sprawling and flapping as the water swirled and seethed and gurgled.

'Hey look, Mr Reilly!' Milton cried. 'I'm swimming!'

Now was not the time for congratulations. We'd been saved from drowning, but we still had to get out of there. 'Hang on to me, kid,' I shouted and I started to climb. The chain was wet and so were my hands. I don't know how we got out without falling back, but we did. I flopped exhausted on the side like a beached dogfish.

I was soaked, but the water just seemed to run off Milton. 'Come on,' I said and jumped. I landed with a squelch, to be joined seconds later by Milton.

'What do we do now,
Mr Reilly?'

'I don't know kid.' It was true.
'If only I'd looked at that map before your rotten
uncle took it I'd know where to go,' I said. I looked
at Milton. He was beaming all over his face.

'It's all right, Mr Reilly,' he said. 'I memorised it.'

I looked at him, stupid with gratitude. 'Kid,' I
said, 'you're incredible — truly incredible. Well
don't just stand there — lead on!

This case was certainly broadening my horizons. I was going places that I never even knew existed. How Toad's gang had got a whole train up here I couldn't begin to guess. I was having trouble even getting myself up. Finally we reached flat ground.

'This is it, Mr Reilly,' Milton whispered. 'Through that gap.'

We crept through the gap and looked around.
This place was spooky. It looked as if no one had

been up here for years. Except for the footprints in the dust. 'Drake,' I breathed.

'The train should be over there.' Milton pointed. 'Behind that big tree.'

Keeping ourselves hidden, we inched around till we could see beyond the fallen tree. And then suddenly, there it was.

Twisted and buckled like some crazy tin snake, it lay where it had lain for years, waiting to be found. The legend made real. The Toad Treasure Train!

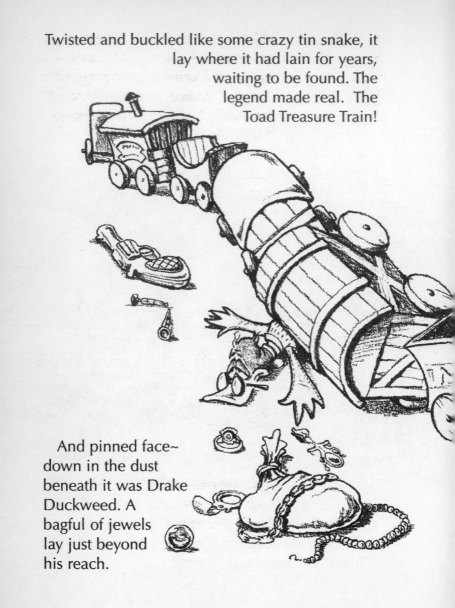

And pinned face~down in the dust beneath it was Drake Duckweed. A bagful of jewels lay just beyond his reach.

Someone should have told him that knowing where treasure lies and getting your mitts on it, are two different things. In his hurry to stuff a bag with jewels and get away, Drake obviously hadn't noticed how precariously balanced the carriages were. As he had been making his getaway, one of the trucks had over-balanced, trapping him.

At first I thought he was a gonner, but then I heard a groan.

'Uncle Drake?' Milton said softly. The kid really was a one-off. After all this wicked uncle had done, his nephew still felt sorry for him.

Duckweed looked over. 'Help me,' he groaned. 'Please. Help me. I can't move.'

Milton rushed over and I followed. Using whatever came to hand we levered and heaved. 'Grab that stick,' I said.

Milton dragged it over and together we heaved. The truck didn't move much, but it was enough. Drake wriggled free and scrambled to his feet. 'OK, Milton,' I gasped. 'Let her go!' With a screech of twisting metal, the truck dropped back. We turned.

'Thank you, Reilly,' Drake said. 'And now I'd be grateful if you'd put your hands up and move over there.'

I was getting very familiar with this routine. 'Better do as he says, kid,' I said.

'Not him!' Drake sneered. 'He's coming with me! Pick up that bag, Milton!' The kid did as he was told, staggering under the weight of Drake's ill-gotten gains. Drake grabbed the collar of Milton's sailor suit and began to back away. 'Look out for that tree, Duckweed,' I called out.

Drake laughed. 'Really, Reilly! Do you expect me to fall for an old trick like— '

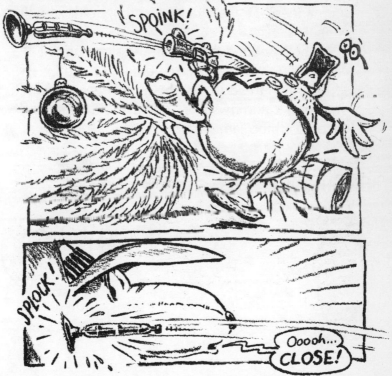

I threw myself at him, knocking the gun away along the ground.

We wrestled, as Milton watched helplessly. Now I could see how Tin Pot Ted had wound up in such a mess. Drake Duckweed fought like a wild animal.

We both spotted the gun at the same time. I dived for it, but Drake caught my foot and I went sprawling in the dust. By the time I'd struggled to my feet, I found myself staring at a view that had become all too familiar.

Drake was breathing hard and looking ruffled. 'I was going to let you go, Reilly,' he wheezed. 'But you'd only come after me. Wouldn't you?'

'I guarantee it!' I said.

'Then that settles it!' he concluded. 'Goodbye, Mr Reilly!'

I wasn't going to let him have the last word. 'Drake!' I said, as he levelled the gun at me. 'You're a low-down yellow—'

'Duck, Mr Reilly!' Milton screamed.

It must have taken all Milton's strength to swing that bag. Drake went flying past me and slammed into the side of one of the trucks he had so recently emptied. He stood there for a moment and for that split second I wondered if he was going to come at us again. Then, like a slow-motion film, his eyes rolled up and he rolled over.

Milton waddled across. 'Mr Reilly,' he said, in a small, shocked voice. 'Is he . . .'

'It's OK, kid,' I smiled. 'He's sleeping. I guess all those jewels just went to his head. Here, help me with him.' Together we bundled Drake into the open truck and fastened the door. I straightened up and put a big paw around Milton's shoulder. 'Nice work,' I said. 'Partner!'

Milton J. Duckweed's face lit up in a million kilowatt grin.

Chapter 9

'Well,' said McWheely, 'Drake Duckweed is going to be in the slammer for a long, long time.' We were waiting for another train. This one was going to take Milton away.

'Officer McWheely,' Milton asked, 'could I visit Uncle Drake sometimes?'

'Sure,' the big cop replied. 'But are you sure you want to?'

'If I know Milton, he'll want to,' I said. That kid never ceased to amaze me. I turned to him. 'What are you going to do now, Milt?'

'Officer McWheely's managed to track down an aunt of mine,' Milton said. 'Jemima.'

'Is she OK?'

'She has no criminal record, as far as I know!'

The train arrived. 'Well, Milt,' I said as he waddled aboard, 'I'm going to miss you.'

'I'll miss you too, Mr Reilly. Maybe when we meet again, I'll be a real detective.'

'In my book kid, you already are.'

'Thanks, Mr Reilly,' he said and, as the train pulled away, I saw a big tear roll down his cheek.

'What a sweet little duck,' Miss Teers sobbed.

'Yeah,' I said. 'I always did like him.'

'But, Mr Reilly,' Charley Taiwan said, 'I thought you said he was a— OW!'

'Sorry, Charley. Did I step on your foot there?'

105

I watched the train until it disappeared around the corner.

Another case closed.

Dumpty invited me back to the Wendy House, but I needed to be alone. I walked back to my little shoebox.

All my stuff had been returned and yet it seemed a little empty somehow.

Then I realised what was wrong. There was a little Milton-shaped hole in it.

I know how it feels, I thought and settled down to get some sleep.

THE END